**Jessica Souhami** studied at the Central School of Art and Design, and
went on to set up a touring shadow puppet company, featuring music and
a storyteller. She is internationally acclaimed for her folk-tale retellings,
bringing some of the world's greatest stories to a young audience. Her many
books for Frances Lincoln include *Foxy!*, *Honk! Honk! Hold Tight!*, *Sausages*, *The Sticky
Doll Trap*, *The Little Little House*, *Old MacDonald*, *No Dinner!*, *The Leopard's Drum* –
the classic West-African tale which has just celebrated its twentieth anniversary –
and *The Strongest Boy in the World*. Jessica lives in north London.

To Gulzar Kanji

# Rama and the Demon King

## An Ancient Tale from India

Retold and illustrated by Jessica Souhami

Frances Lincoln
Children's Books

This is the story of a brave and good prince called Rama, who should have been the happiest of men.

After all, he was the King's favourite son. He had a dear wife called Sita, and he had the best of friends in his brother, Lakshman.

And all the people in the kingdom loved him.

Well, all but one...
and that was his jealous stepmother.
She HATED Rama.
And she planned to get rid of him forever.
So she set a trap...

Rama's wicked stepmother went to the King.

"Long ago," she said, "I saved your life and you promised to grant me any wish. Now I want you to send Rama into the forest for fourteen years."

The King was horrified. The forest was full of terrible demons. But what could he do?

A king MUST keep his promise.

With a broken heart, he sent Rama away.

But Sita and Lakshman would not let Rama go alone. So that very day, all three left the palace to face the dangers of the forest together.

In the forest, news of Rama's exile spread fast.

The demons hated anyone good and they were spoiling for a fight. As soon as Rama, Sita and Lakshman appeared, the demons attacked them gleefully.

But both princes were brilliant fighters. They fought back bravely and killed thousands of demons until at last there was peace in the forest.

Rama, Sita and Lakshman built a house, gathered fruit and berries for food and lived a quiet and simple life among the forest animals.

BUT it was not to last.

Far away, in a magnificent palace on the island of Lanka, lived Ravana, the ten-headed king of all the demons.

He was evil and proud.

"No one can defeat me," he boasted. "No one is stronger than me. No one is more cunning. No one knows as much magic."

He smiled ten horrible smiles.

One day, a messenger arrived from India and told Ravana how Rama and Lakshman had killed thousands of his demons.

"WHAAAAT!" his ten mouths screeched.

And he quivered with rage.

Ravana leapt into his magic chariot and flew to India. There he hid in a tree, ready to pounce on Rama and Lakshman.

But when he caught sight of Sita he stopped short, dazzled by her beauty.

"She must be my queen!" he muttered. "I'll steal her from Rama and leave him broken-hearted. Serve him right for killing my demons!"

And his ten brains buzzed with evil schemes.

This is what Ravana did.

He sent a magic deer into the forest, a golden creature which enchanted Sita. But whenever she tried to stroke it, it moved just out of reach.

Rama offered to catch it for her.

"Lakshman," he said, "look after Sita while I'm gone. There may still be demons about."

And he followed the deer until they both disappeared from view.

All was quiet.

Suddenly, Sita and Lakshman heard a cry.

"Help me! Help me, Lakshman!"

It sounded just like Rama.

Now, what should Lakshman do?

He could not look for Rama. He had to protect Sita.

But Sita said, "Leave me, Lakshman, and rescue Rama.
I'm safe here. Hurry!"

Then Lakshman ran as fast as he could towards the voice.

But, of course, it was not Rama calling.

It was a fiendish trick of Ravana's.

And now Sita was alone.

Wicked Ravana swooped down and carried her off in his magic chariot.

Meanwhile, Lakshman found Rama unhurt. With horror, the brothers realised they had been tricked.

They raced back to Sita.

But she was gone.

Rama was desolate.

The two brothers looked all over India for Sita.
Their search seemed hopeless.

Then, one day, they came to the land of the monkeys.
There they met Hanuman, the leader of the monkey army,
and told him their story.

"Ravana has taken Sita," said Hanuman. "We saw them
flying towards his palace on the island of Lanka."

"But how can we reach her?" asked Rama. "The sea round
Lanka is full of monsters."

"I think I can help you," said Hanuman. "My father is Vayu, the Wind God, and so I can fly like the wind! I will find Sita for you."

Rama and Lakshman were astonished.

"Take my ring," said Rama. "When you find Sita, give it to her so she will know I sent you. Good luck."

And Hanuman flew across the treacherous sea to Lanka.

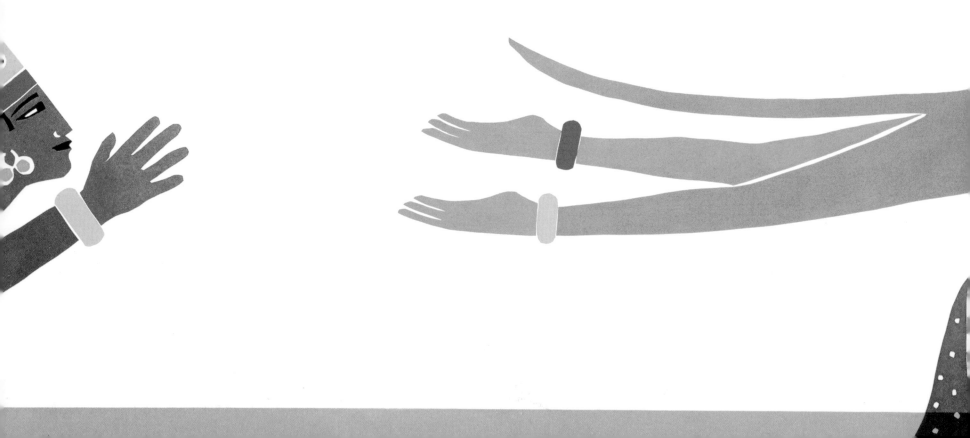

Hanuman found Sita imprisoned in Ravana's garden.

He gave her Rama's ring.

"I'm so glad to see you," she cried. "I've refused to become Ravana's queen. If I don't change my mind, he says he will chop me into little pieces and eat me up for breakfast!"

"Be brave, Sita," whispered Hanuman. "We will be back for you soon."

Hanuman returned to Rama with his news, and the monkey army prepared for battle.

They began by building an amazing bridge which stretched right across the sea from India to Lanka.

Then the army, led by Rama, Lakshman and Hanuman, marched across it!

Ravana's demon army was waiting for them on Lanka.

A terrible battle began.

The demons tried all their evil tricks.

Some used magic arrows that turned into poisonous snakes. Others became invisible, so that the monkeys only saw a sea of whirling weapons. There were giant demons with enormous strength and demons who could move at the speed of light.

But Rama, Lakshman and the monkey army stood firm and, after many days of fierce fighting, the demons were defeated.

BUT THEN...

Ravana appeared, his twenty eyes blazing.

"Ha, Rama!" he sneered. "You know you cannot beat ME!"

Rama was silent. He slowly raised his bow and released a magic arrow.

It found its own way to Ravana. It pierced his evil body. Ravana was DEAD.

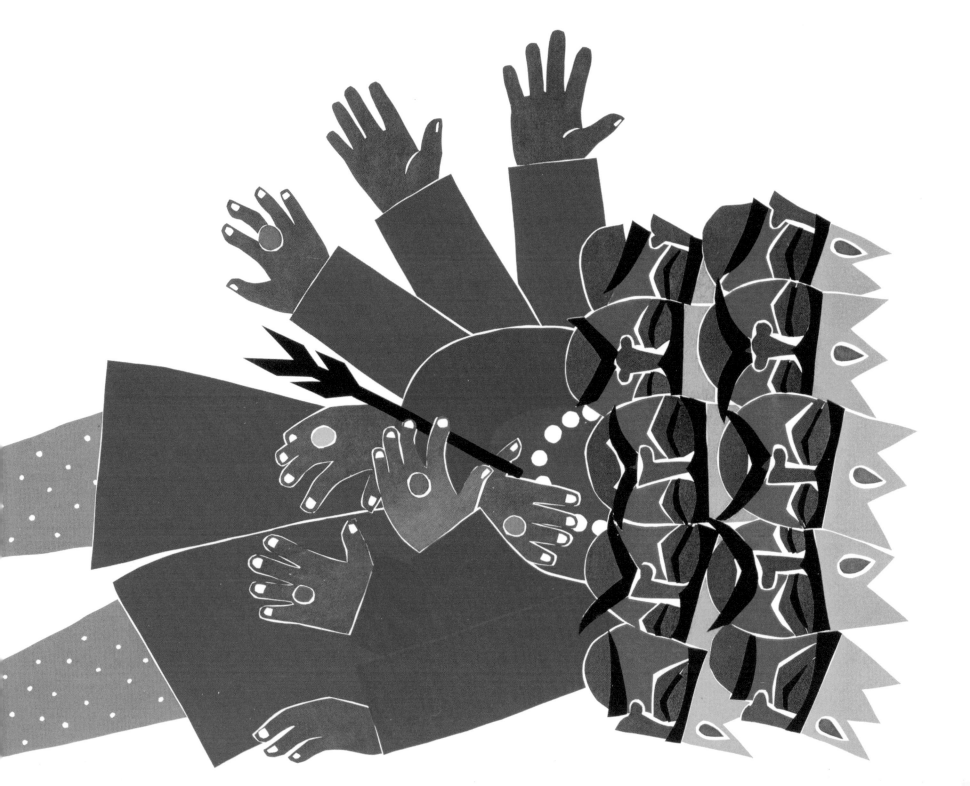

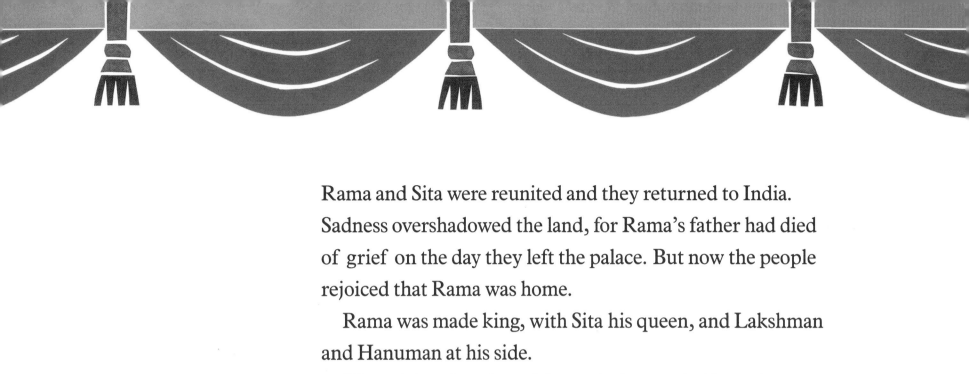

Rama and Sita were reunited and they returned to India. Sadness overshadowed the land, for Rama's father had died of grief on the day they left the palace. But now the people rejoiced that Rama was home.

Rama was made king, with Sita his queen, and Lakshman and Hanuman at his side.

The celebrations lasted for a whole month. Even the stepmother who had plotted against Rama was invited.

Rama ruled wisely and well.

The land became fruitful, and at last the kingdom was free from all evil.

The story of Rama, who rescues his wife, Sita, from the Demon King,
has been told in India for thousands of years and is said to confer
a blessing on all who hear it.

The legend may have been based on historical fact.
It passed from person to person until, in about 400 B.C., the poet Valmiki
wrote the *Ramayana*. Almost every regional language in India has its own version.
and the story has spread throughout south-east Asia. Heroic saga, love story
and symbolic account of the battle between good and evil, the *Ramayana*
has inspired countless works of art and literature.

First published in Great Britain and in the USA in 1997 by
Frances Lincoln Children's Books, 74-77 White Lion Street, London N1 9PF
www.franceslincoln.com

This paperback edition first published in Great Britain and in the USA in 2015

A catalogue record for this book is available from the British Library.

ISBN 978-1-84780-660-4

Illustrated with collage of Ingres papers hand-painted with watercolour inks and graphite pencil

Printed in China

1 3 5 7 9 8 6 4 2

# ALSO BY JESSICA SOUHAMI
## PUBLISHED BY FRANCES LINCOLN CHILDREN'S BOOKS

### The Strongest Boy in the World
Jessica Souhami

Kaito is very strong – stronger than all the other boys in his village.
No one can beat him at wrestling, and one day he sets out to the city to try
his skill at the world-famous Sumo wrestling tournament.

'This is a beautiful retelling of an old tale, enriched by action-packed
illustrations that capture the humour and bring the story and
characters to life.' — *English Association*

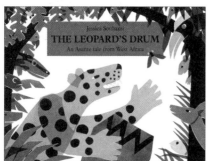

### The Leopard's Drum
### An Asante Tale from West Africa
Jessica Souhami

Osebo the leopard has a fine drum, a huge drum, a 'magnificent' drum.
All the animals covet Osebo's drum, but he won't let anyone else have it,
not even Nyame, the Sky-God. So, Nyame offers a big reward to the animal
that brings him the drum. All try – the monkey, the elephant, even the
python – and all fail. Can a very small tortoise succeed in outwitting the
boastful leopard?

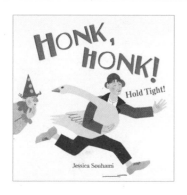

### Honk Honk! Hold Tight!
Jessica Souhami

In this funny folktale, a princess will not laugh. Her father says he will give her
hand in marriage to the man who can make her laugh, so one boy plus a golden
goose set off to the palace to try their luck... As they go along, the animals and
people they meet all try to steal one of the golden goose's feathers – and they
stick fast to the goose. "*Honk! Honk! Hold Tight!*" says the boy, and the whole
parade soon ends up at the palace. What will the princess do?

Frances Lincoln titles are available from all good bookshops.
You can also buy books and find out more about your favourite titles,
authors and illustrators on our website: www.franceslincoln.com